Angie Pfeiffer

The Golden Sunstone

AF194078

Angie Pfeiffer

The Golden Sunstone

For Charlotte and Jakob, for Leo, Lia,
Marie and Max.

English first edition

© 2020
by Angie Pfeiffer
All rights reserved.
Production and publishing:
Books on Demand GmbH,
Norderstedt
ISBN: 9783751935401

Chapter 1
Tavalu and Tuvala

Far, far away, at the ends of the earth, there were once two islands. They lay in the middle of the largest of all oceans. There was no land around them, only water and sky as far as the eye could see. Although the islands were close to each other, they were very different from each other, because one island was quite big and the other one very small.

The big island was called Tavalu.
Many people lived there. All day long they were busy with work, walking here and there and trying to be on time. If they had to wait, they quickly became impatient and got in a bad mood. First, they tapped their feet, then they stared into space.

Finally, they started to shout at the top of their voices because they had so much to do and their time would be wasted now that they could earn a lot of money in the meantime.

Tavalu was ruled by a King who spent the whole day ruling. Day after day he stood at his desk, taking notes and thinking up new laws. Often, when he felt that he had not done enough, he reigned until well into the night. He had learned this from his father, who had also been a very busy King. "Rain brings blessings and what you can do today, don't put off until tomorrow, my dear Regulus", he often told his son. King Regulus had remembered this saying exactly and kept to it. After all, he had to think for his subjects and decide who was right in case of disputes. That was hard work. Sometimes, when he happened to have time, he loved to stand on the pinnacle of his palace and watch his subjects busily on their way.

If by mistake his eyes fell onto the small island, which was a few miles from Tavalu, he shook his head. "How can one be so lazy!" he exclaimed.

The small island was called Tuvala.
In the Tavalusian and Tuvalese language this means nothing but towel. That was because Tuvala was really small and narrow. The people were fishermen who went out to sea at night and laid out their nets. In the early morning they came back to the harbour of Tuvala. After getting back home safely, they were tired, of course, because they had been up all night.
They lay down comfortably in their beds and slept until the afternoon. After getting up they had a late breakfast in peace.
In general, the people on the small island were content. They did everything calmly.

13

No one could think of any particular hurry. If they had to wait, they made themselves comfortable, put their feet up or took a nap. Because no one wanted to earn much money, the people of Tuvala had time to sing, dance or play together. You could say that people simply had more time to live.

Tuvala was not governed at all. King Regulus had no authority in Tuvalu and there was no King of his own on the small island. Everybody did pretty much what they wanted. Everyone got along fine. After all, nobody had more than the other. No one was jealous of the other. Whenever there was a dispute, everyone tried to find a solution. If that didn't succeed, they went to the ancient Yuin, who was a wise man and therefore always knew what to do. He had lived for ages in a hut near the beach. Even the oldest people on Tavalu could not remember that Yuin had once been a little boy. People said that he was a great sorcerer, but no one knew it for sure. Most of the time Yuin sat peacefully in front of his hut and listened to the wind and waves. In the morning, when all the fishermen came back from their sea journey, he mostly got a big fish for his daily meal, because Yuin could not go out to fish anymore. He was far too old for that. Then he gave the fishermen a friendly nod and thanked them.

In the afternoons the children often came to Yuin's house. They sat around him in a circle. He loved to tell them stories about the wind whispering in the trees and the waves murmuring on the shore. Wind and waves had seen so much already and told this to Yuin. And he told the children.

Amali, a little girl, was especially fond of listening to Yuin's stories.

Sometimes, when the other children didn't feel like sitting quietly and listening to the stories and preferred to romp and climb, she liked to come to Yuin alone. She sat down next to him and just waited, because he knew hundreds of stories and one of them, he definitely told Amali.

The inhabitants of the two islands did nothing bad or good to each other. They simply did not care about each other and lived peacefully side by side. The people on the big island were happy because everything was well arranged and they always had something to do. They liked having King Regulus ruling them.

On the small island people were happy that they could do what they wanted and nobody was telling them what to do.

Therefore, the people on Tavalu and Tuvala lived happily for many, many years.

I am sure that this would have gone on forever if the big ship had not docked with them. If only the captain had overlooked the two islands and sailed past! But unfortunately, he did not.

Chapter 2
A strange visit

One morning Yuin was sitting outside his hut as usual. He watched the sunrise and was happy that it would be a beautiful day. Suddenly he frowned. What was that black spot back there on the horizon?? He tried to look very carefully. He shielded his eyes from the bright sun by holding his hand over his eyebrows.

In fact, the spot quickly grew larger and took shape. It was a large sailing ship which was approaching fast. It stopped in the middle of the bay, right in front of the beach where Yuin's hut was located. A dinghy was lowered into the water and several people got into it, some of whom started to paddle. Soon the boat set course for the beach. Astonished Yuin looked at it all, because no one had ever visited the island of Tuvalu before. He could not imagine what the strangers wanted on here. And he had never seen such a big sailing ship before.

Finally, the dinghy had arrived at the beach. The men jumped out and pushed it onto the sand so that it couldn't sail away. Then they looked around and discovered Yuin, who was still sitting quietly in front of his hut.

They came straight towards him. In front of them went a small, fat man who had squeezed his belly into a tight uniform jacket. His jacket was glowing red and had all kinds of golden tassels on the shoulders, reaching down to the elbows. His trousers were in shiny boots. At his side dangled a dangerous looking sabre.

The men who marched behind him also wore uniforms, but they were not red, they were simply dark blue. And they did not have tassels either.

"What a strange company", Yuin thought. Because he was a polite man, he didn't let on and slowly got up. "Welcome to Tuvala", he said loud and clear.

The men stopped. Their leader swayed up and down on his knees and inspected Yuin from top to bottom. "Who are you. What are you doing? Are there other people here? Where are they? We are accustomed to being greeted by the inhabitants of the islands that we honour with our visit", he buzzed.

"I just greeted you", Yuin explained amusedly. He found the little fat man quite funny. "The others must not have seen you yet. They are all asleep at this time of day."

"Well, well. They are sleeping? Lazy blighters, aren't they? Very well. Where is your King's palace? I will pay him a visit and inform him that his subjects are inattentive and sleepy. After all, I am General Brigadus, emissary of the emperor of Mesopotunia. His Imperial Highness Raj the Fifth will be furious that I am not accorded respect here. This could have dire consequences."

Yuin shook his head. He was wondering more and more about this person. "There's no King here, let alone a palace. I've never heard of a Raj before. Neither the first nor the fifth. What is this all about? You just come here and make a fuss that's really strange. The best you can do is to leave right now with your showboat. You have no business here. If you're looking for a King, you must go to our neighbouring island, Tavalu. Regulus rules there. I don't know if it's the first, the second or the fifth. Don't bother me now. Our people have earned their just sleep." After these words he sat down again in front of his hut and didn't pay attention to the strange group.

General Brigadus went bright red in the face. "What impertinence is this. What do you think you're doing, old man? Talking to me like that! I think it would be best if we didn't stay here any longer. Let's take a closer look at the neighbouring island and its King. He probably rules on that impossible island, too. I'll tell him what's going on. Then you can dress warmly."

"I don't need to dress warmly. It's sunny here all year round", Yuin grinned after him and decided to take another nap himself.

Chapter 3
General Brigadus knows better

While Yuin made himself comfortable and soon fell asleep, General Brigadus let himself be rowed back to his sailing ship. Here he decided to sail to the neighbouring island immediately. There, he wanted to go to the palace of this Regulus and complain to him. A curious King it was, who let his people sleep in broad daylight.

And so it happened. No sooner had the sailing ship anchored in the port of Tavalu the general set off.

"Pull on the oars, men", he urged the soldiers who were rowing the dinghy. "I want to meet the King of this island as soon as possible. It's about time someone showed him how to govern sensibly." He was panting through his nose. "Pah, subjects who sleep instead of working. Where else can you get that?"

Right by the harbour, on a hill, stood the palace of King Regulus. A path led up, which General Brigadus climbed, puffing. When he reached the top, he took out a large checkered handkerchief and wiped the sweat from his brow. Then he knocked violently on the palace door.

Nothing moved.

"This King Regulus also seems to be sleeping. No wonder his subjects are so lazy", he grumbled and knocked at the door once more.

"At last!" growled the general, as the door opened creaking a little. An old man, wearing a plain uniform, peeped through the gap.

"Yes?", he asked stretched out.

General Brigadus examined him from top to bottom.

"So that's the slovenly King of these sleepy islands", he thought.

But of course, he didn't utter the thought aloud. Instead, he asked, "Are you King Regulus?"

"No", the man replied.

"No?" Now the general was stunned.

"No!", the man reiterated.

Who were all these strange people on these islands? General Brigadus shook his head.

Wherever he had docked on his voyage, people had treated him with great reverence. The Kings of the different countries had greeted him kindly and respectfully. After all, he was the emissary of the great and powerful Emperor of Mesopotunia! One could not be too careful with great and powerful emperors and their emissaries. But that did not seem to have searched these puny islands. The people here still had a lot to learn!

The General sighed. "So, you are not the King of these islands", he said. "I want to see the King. You will bring him here or take me to him. Who are you, anyway?"

"Oops", said the man, and it sounded as if he was burping loudly.

Now it became too colourful for the general. "Oops! How dare you! I am General Brigadus. I am the emissary of the mighty emperor of Mesopotunia! Don't burp me, take me to your King immediately. If you value your life", he roared and drew his sabre.

The man took a step back. "Pardon", he said calmly and fearlessly. "You have misunderstood. My name is Oops. I am the first minister of King Regulus. Now you'd better put your sabre away or you might hurt somebody or cut yourself."

The general was so astounded that his counterpart was not afraid at all that he put the sabre back into the belt without any objection. "What a strange name. All right, I don't want to be like that today. Now take me to your King... Mr. Minister."

The old man opened the door a little wider.

"I can ask if Her Majesty is free to receive you. You must know that King Regulus is always very busy. After all, he must reign", he explained.

At the same time, he meant the General to follow him.

Chapter 4
Chocolate tax

King Regulus sat in his throne room and pondered. He had wrinkled his forehead from all the effort. Although he had enough to do with directing Tavalu, he had been dissatisfied lately. He didn't know exactly what was the reason for that himself. Perhaps he should pass a new law? That would probably keep him busy for a while. But what kind of law would it be? It so happens that Tavalu already had all kinds of laws, so everything was well regulated. A new tax? Yes, that was one option worth thinking about.

A knock interrupted the King's deliberations. The first minister put his head through the door to the throne room. "Your Majesty, I hate to disturb you. I know only too well that you are occupied with important matters..."

"Indeed, I am", the King interrupted him. "But now you've interrupted my thoughts anyway, my dear Oops. Just as I was about to devise a new tax for my subjects. So - what's so urgent?"

"Well", the minister stepped from one leg to the other.

"'Well' what? I don't have all day", King Regulus grumbled and realised again that he was becoming discontented.

The door was ripped open and General Brigadus stormed into the throne room. "With respect, before this minister with that funny burp gets to the point, I'd better introduce myself", he boasted, saluted snappily and clicked his heels together.

"I am General Brigadus. Emissary of the great and powerful Emperor Raj the Fifth of Mesopotunia. I'm on an important mission."

For a moment the King stood there with his mouth open, because an emissary of any Emperor or King had never come to Tavalu. and certainly not on an important mission. He cleared his throat. "My dear General..." He faltered because he didn't understand the name of the emissary.

The General seemed to have guessed. "Brigadus, General Brigadus of Meso-potunia", he said loud and slow. "As sorry as I am, my dear King Regulus, I must immediately make some criti-cisms at this point. There is something very wrong on these islands."

"Hear, hear", said Minister Oops in surprise.

"Hear, hear", echoed the King amazed.

"Yes! not at all", clarified the general. " Where else are people who sleep in broad daylight when they should be working. The whole island seems to me to be deserted. Only one old man on the beach is awake. But I think he's gone back to sleep after talking to me."

"That's not true at all! My subjects sleep at night and not during the day", exclaimed King Regulus.

To be on the safe side, he quickly ran to the window to make sure that the people outside were really walking back and forth. Relieved, he realized that this was the case. "Look for your-self. People are on the move. You must be mistaken, General!"

Minister Oops nodded. "That's right, only hardworking people live on Tava-lu."

General Brigadus stood beside the King at the window. In fact, the people in the harbour seemed to be quite busy, he hadn't paid any attention to that before. Suddenly, something occurred to him. " Yes, it's quite different here than on the other island, too. You should go there and see how things are going, Mr. King."

King Regulus shook his head. "Now I understand. You don't mean Tavalu, but the small island next door. That's Tuvala. Tavalu and Tuvala have nothing to do with each other, except that they are neighbouring islands. The people of Tuvala are a very peculiar people. Fish-ermen who go out to sea at night and do nothing else. They sleep when they want. Otherwise, they spend their days dancing and singing. They don't care about money. We here in Tavalu cannot understand this, because we like to work all day and go to bed early in the evening, because we have to get up early in the morning to continue working."

General Brigadus slapped the King on the back, which made him flinch violently. "That's right. Work is half the battle. So said my father, who had one more star on his uniform than I have." Here Brigadus pointed to his shoulder pads, on which two small golden stars were emblazoned. "But I will soon get the third star when I have completed my important mission", he added. "Have you ever thought of bringing civilsation to the people on this small island?"

"Huh?", Minister Oops could be heard.

"What do you mean?" asked King Regulus, stunned.

"Well, it looks as if these Tuvalese are pure savages. They just do whatever they want. That's probably because they don't have a King to tell them what to do. This would be an opportunity for you, Your Majesty, to declare the island your territory. After all, it's right next door. Then you can teach the people there how to make life more beautiful."

King Regulus scratched his head. "It's not a bad idea. Lately I've been thinking back and forth about what to do anyway. I've even been considering introducing a new tax. It just hasn't occurred to me yet what it's for. Of course, it would be a task to bring order to the neighbouring island and make the people happier. But what do I do if the people of Tuvala don't want that? After all, they have been fishermen on their island for ages.

"Pah", snorted the general. "If they don't want that, you'll just have to convince them of their luck. I would put my sailing ship at your disposal and give you sound advice, my dear King Regulus. Together we should be able to bring these stubborn fishermen to their senses."

"Where would you take them?", Minister Oops asked in a distraught manner. He had listened with growing concern. What this Brigadus was telling the King seemed to be very dangerous to him.

Coldly smiling, the general turned around. "You are still here. Are you not the King's first minister? Then you should have advised King Regulus to add the neighbouring island to his kingdom long ago." Here he turned to the King again. "United Kingdom of Tavalu and Tuvala. That sounds good, Your Majesty, doesn't it?!"

The King nodded enthusiastically. "That sounds very, very good!" He greeted his first minister with a cool look. "You could have come up with this idea earlier. What's the point of having a first minister if a Mesopotamian general has to come and tell me how to expand my kingdom?"

"Uhm, but so far, everything's been fine as it is. Without extensions of any kind, Majesty", the Minister murmured astonished.

"Was it though?", General Brigadus intervened. "That shows you have no idea, Minister Oops. Obviously, King Regulus is not pleased. Otherwise, he wouldn't have so much to think about. Especially not over new taxes. Which reminds me: has your island introduced a tax on chocolate?"

"No, indeed there is no such thing", the King said thoughtfully. "One might consider introducing a tax on chocolate."

"King Regulus, what is there to think about? Take the tax directly, Your Majesty."

Minister Oops shook his head sadly. "Children especially like to taste chocolate. If there is a chocolate tax, chocolate will become more expensive and parents may no longer be able to buy chocolate for their children. That would be mean."

"You again", General Brigadus ran at him. "If the little brats whine and cry enough, their parents will go on buying chocolate, just to have their peace and quiet. I know that from experience. In Mesopotunia there has long been a chocolate tax and a tax on sweets and a tax on biscuits. But here, I would advise starting with one tax. When people get used to it, you can introduce other taxes on sweets."

"I disagree completely. Chocolate tax, where can you find that...", the minister exclaimed indignantly.

"Really, Oops. What's the matter with you? The idea is quite excellent. It's better if you go now. I want to speak to the General alone. I don't like it when you interfere."

The King pointed strictly to the exit door.

Minister Oops had no choice but to leave the throne room. He shook his head again. A chocolate tax and simply add Tuvala Island to the kingdom? What crazy things that strange general told the King! He decided to have a quiet talk with King Regulus in a quiet hour.

Chapter 5
King Regulus is taking a decision

"Well, we got rid of him, my dear King Regulus", said the general, as soon as Minister Oops had closed the door from the outside. "What a stupid first minister you have. He can't think of a single thing. This person is perhaps good as a scribe, perhaps as your secretary, but as a minister he is a failure. What other ministers are there with you? Are they on their toes at least?"

"There are no other ministers. Oops is my first and only one", the King explained. "So far we have not needed other ministers here at Tavalu."

"Yes, so far. But if you want to rule the United Kingdoms of Tavalu and Tuvalu in the future, you need help, my friend. After all, you must look after the savages on the neighbouring island. I can stay here and help you for now, but at some point, I must leave. After all, I'm on assignment from Emperor Raj the Fifth."

The general stretched with dignity, which made his jacket stretch over his huge belly. The linen of his jacket groaned and the buttons threatened to burst off. With glance, King Regulus wondered whether he should take cover. If the buttons came off, they would shoot through the throne room like bullets! Not that he'd be hit in the head by a button. That could cause long-term damage. But before the King could take cover behind his throne, the general had stopped stretching. The linen relaxed a bit and King Regulus took a breath.

"What would you do if you wanted to add Tuvala to my kingdom? As a general, you must have some idea", he said.

Brigadus nodded. "But of course. I have fought many battles for my emperor."

Regulus flinched. "Oh, no. No battles, please. I don't want that at all."

"Hey, hey, don't be so sensitive, Your Majesty. I was just saying that. We can deal with this little island next door without fighting. What about your fleet? Do you have any ships? Big ships, I mean. If that is not the case, I'm happy to put my magnificent sailing ship at your disposal. We could sail this one over to Tuvalu. People will be impressed when they see this ship. Then we will go ashore and you will declare the island part of your kingdom. Probably the islanders will be happy that they now belong to the United Kingdom of Tavalu and Tuvala and are ruled by such a great King as you are. You will then explain to your new subjects what you expect of them. Done." Here the general ran out of breath. He took a deep breath.

"That's it?", asked King Regulus astounded, because he had not imagined the whole thing to be so easy.

"That's it!", replied the General.

"But...", said the King, for he was still worried that the people of Tuvala might not want to be ruled by him.

The General once again gave him a strong slap on the shoulder. "No buts, my dear King. If your new subjects are unruly, then we shall see. Then we must make them understand that they must obey. Sending a few soldiers to them can often work wonders."

"Do you really think it's that simple?" the King thought and rubbed his shoulder.

"You can trust me, Sire. Before they have understood what is going on, the people will already be your subjects. They will get used to it very quickly, and what you are used to, you don't want to change anymore."

Slowly King Regulus sat down on his throne chair. "Then we will sail to Tuvala as quickly as possible."

"Very well, immediately", the General explained.

"So be it," King Regulus replied happily. Arm in arm, they left the throne room.

Chapter 6
Minister Oops goes to Tuvala

Minister Oops was a loyal subject of King Regulus. Already his father had been the first minister of Regulus' father and had always advised him well. So being a minister was a tradition in the Oops family.

Today however Minister Oops did something that he could never have imagined. He listened at the door to the throne room. He was a little ashamed of it, because listening at doors, as we all know, is not something you should do. Nevertheless, the minister pressed his ear very firmly to the keyhole, to understand every word the King and General Brigadus said.

What he heard horrified the minister. Surely the King could not simply make the neighbouring island part of his kingdom without asking the people whether they wanted it at all. Oops doubted that the people of Tuvala wanted to be ruled by King Regulus. What good would that do? So far, everything had worked out well on Tuvala and that without a King.

When he noticed that the King and General Brigadus had finished talking, Minister Oops quickly ran out of the palace. For one thing, he was afraid that the King might notice that he had been listening at the door. On the other hand, because he had decided to warn the people on the small island, haste was called for, because it sounded, as if the King and the general were about to sail to Tuvala.

It was good that the palace was close to the harbour. Oops could walk directly to his sailing boat and get it ready for take-off. Soon he was on his way to Tuvala.

Nobody on the small island suspected what was about to happen. It was afternoon. The fishermen had slept in and were now having late breakfast, as they did every day.

Yuin was sitting outside his hut. A group of children had gathered around him and waited anxiously for the story he would tell them. Amali sat close to Yuin. She too looked at him expectantly. But before Yuin could start the story, a boat approached. In it stood a person who was waving excitedly.

Yuin thought out loud and stood up to take a closer look at the new arrival. "Why is the person on the boat so fidgety? The sea is calm, it's a sunny afternoon, and the boat doesn't look as if it's sinking."

"He's from Tavalu! People are always excited there, my mum said", Amali explained.

Yuin nodded to her. "That's right. On the big island, they swarm around all day long. In the evening they are tired and don't even have time to tell each other stories or sing a song together.

But if they like that, we shouldn't worry. So, let's let the man fidget around in his boat if it pleases him."

He sat down again and began to tell his story: "Once upon a time there was a very special stone. It was the Golden Sunstone. As its name suggests, the stone shone as if it were made of gold when the sun caressed it with its rays. But that was not the only reason it was special."

"Hello, can you hear me? I need to talk to you", a voice sounded. The boat had come close to shore by now. The man had sat down and was paddling frantically to get to the beach.

"To me?" Yuin asked astonished.

"Yes, with you. It's important!" The stranger, who was none other than Minister Oops, pulled the boat to the beach. Then he walked with big steps towards the small meeting. "It would be better if we talked in private", he explained. "Perhaps we could walk along the beach for a while? If you don't mind."

Yuin looked at him from top to bottom. "Why would I do that? I don't know you. Anyway, I was about to tell the children a story. I don't know if it's more important to talk to you."

"Oh, it's really important. Therefore I will also allow you to address me without my title. That's not really usual. After all, I am the first minister of King

Regulus. Oops is my name. Minister Oops. Please come on." Excited, the minister grabbed Yuin's arm and pulled it a little.

Yuin was outraged. "Stop it!" he shouted and pulled his arm to safety. "If it's so important, I'll go with you. You're always complaining, Minister Oops. Children, I don't think there'll be any story today. I'll tell you tomorrow, all right?"

The children grumbled a little, because they had been looking forward to a new story. 'The Golden Sunstone', that sounded exciting. They decided to play on the beach and pretend that they had just found the Golden Sunstone.

Minister Oops and Yuin left together in another direction. "Tell me what's so important?" Yuin asked.

The minister rubbed the tip of his nose, as he always did when he was thinking or worried. "It's really hard for me. At first, I thought: I can't just go to Tuvala and reveal my King's plans, since I am his first minister. But then..." Oops sighed heavily.

He told Yuin about what had happened today. That General Brigadus had appeared in the palace and disturbed the King's reign. That he had persuaded King Regulus to form the United Kingdom of Tavalu and Tuvala.

"The King wants to sail over to you with this strange general as soon as possible and declare that you belong to the new kingdom from now on. He also wants to tell you what to do and what not to do in the future. General Brigadus doesn't like you sleeping during the day and not working all the time. He has complained to the King about this, though it is none of his business. I thought it would be better if you knew about it."

Yuin had listened quietly to Oop's explanations without interrupting him even once. "I've already met the General in his show-off uniform. He is an unpleasant and conceited man. This morning he moored his sailing ship here and let himself be rowed to the beach. Then he was screaming and yelling. I sent him to you because he was looking for a King. It seems he found him. But that they would both come here now, I didn't think so! What kind of nonsense is this anyway? United Kingdom! We don't need a King and we don't need a kingdom. We'll just tell the King and then he can sail back. Let him find another island for his United Kingdom."

"I hope the King is wise enough to listen to this. That Brigadus has got him all confused with his talk. In fact, Regulus is a good King."

Yuin gave him a friendly nod. "That may well be. Still we don't need a King. We are fishermen and we are content with that. We want to live here in peace. If King Regulus really wants to rule here, then he shouldn't bother us with it. It's kind of you to come specially to warn us. We won't forget that. Now I'm going to the village to talk to the others so they'll know what's going on. Do you want to come with me or would you rather go back to Tavalu? Your King will miss you later."

Minister Oops had not yet thought of this idea. He quickly said goodbye to Yuin and ran back to his boat.

Chapter 7
The United Kingdom
of Tavalu and Tuvala

While Minister Oops made a great effort to return to Tavalu as soon as possible, General Brigadus' sailing ship with the King on board docked in the small port of Tuvala.

"Here we are, your Majesty", Brigadus solemnly declared. "On your new island." He swung both arms far out, almost knocking down one of his soldiers. At the last second, the man jumped aside and made himself safe.

"Hm," during the crossing King Regulus had become uncertain whether he was doing the right thing. Now he was thinking about calling it all off and sailing back. "Perhaps we should sleep on it for a night before proclaiming the United Kingdom", he said tentatively.

"Rubbish", exclaimed General Brigadus, puffing himself up, so that once again there was a danger that the buttons would pop off his jacket. King Regulus took a step backwards as a precaution. "Now, here we are. We will go ashore and explain to the people that from now on they have the honour of being ruled by you. That's it!"

"Do you really think so?" asked the King.

"That is what I mean. Let's go!" With these words the general pushed the King on to the gangplank that his people had already moored at the pier.

Now both stood on shore and looked around in amazement, because nobody cared about them. The fishermen tied their nets or continued to get their boats ready for the evening sail. The women cooked together around a big fire and sang a funny song. The children played as if nothing had happened.

"Hello, everybody, listen!", General Brigadus finally shouted as loud as he could. "King Regulus has something to say."

"Really?" replied one fisherman without interrupting his work. "Then let him do so."

"Yes, and then he can go right back to the ship and go back to where he came from", another added.

"This is an insult to His Majesty", shouted General Brigadus. "How dare you! If your King wants to make a speech, you must all listen carefully."

A man approached General Brigadus and the King. "Why our King? We don't have one and we don't want any King."

General Brigadus examined him closely. "I know you", he exclaimed. "You were on the beach this morning, weren't you?"

"Maybe", Yuin replied. "I see you have found a King. But what are you doing here? And why are you shouting again? It's not good for you to get so upset."

Before General Brigadus could reply, King Regulus spoke up. He had stood there in silence until now because he didn't know what to say. The whole thing seemed a little embarrassing to him.

"Hello, I am King Regulus of Tavalu. You know, the island next door. I came by to say hello. The islands have been next door for so long, and yet you and I barely speak to each other. Isn't that funny? We should talk a lot more. I have a good idea about that. What if we were to form the United Kingdom of Tavalu and Tuvala? That would be great."

Yuin shrugged his shoulders. "What's the use?" The others murmured approvingly. They had listened to what Yuin had learned from Minister Oops. After everyone had thought it over, they decided that Yuin should speak with the King and the general if they actually came to Tuvala.

"Well, then we are united, so to speak. I would of course be King of both empires and would rule them", the King explained.

"We will settle our affairs alone. We do not need a King for that. We don't care whether you rule or not as long as you don't disturb us here on Tuvala with this. Otherwise, you must find another island for your United Kingdom." Yuin turned to the other people. "What do you think?"

"So be it", they cried. "If he insists on a United Kingdom, let him proclaim it", and, "but he must leave us alone here in Tuvalu."

King Regulus and General Brigadus looked at each other in bewilderment. They hadn't expected that. The general shrugged his shoulders. "You should seize the opportunity, Your Majesty", he whispered to the King. "Once this island is part of your kingdom, then we shall see."

"That's right", whispered King Regulus back. He cleared his throat. "So, if you have no objection, I hereby proclaim the United Kingdom of Tavalu and Tuvala. I promise to leave you alone as much as possible, as I am King Regulus." After these words, the King looked around expectantly, for he was sure that his new subjects would throw their hats into the air and cheer him with enthusiasm. But nothing happened. The people went on with their work, the children played as if nothing had happened. Puzzled, the King stopped for a moment and General Brigadus also looked around in amazement. Finally, they both went back to the sailing ship.

"Strange people, my new subjects, I must say", the King remarked.

"Surely they were so overwhelmed by their joy that they could not say any-thing", General Brigadus ventured. "Or they have yet to learn that they must cheer their King. That will come. In any case, the first step has been taken."

Chapter 8
We need a new palace

A few weeks had passed since King Regulus had visited Tuvala. He now reigned on both islands, but there was not much to notice, because he had actually left the people of Tuvala alone until then.

General Brigadus still stood by his side in word and deed. He had made sure that a chocolate tax had indeed been introduced on Tavalu. The people had grumbled, but then they paid the higher price.

Minister Oops was still in office, but the King would not listen to him. The minister often tried to talk to the King when the two of them met in the palace, but King Regulus always waved him off. "Sorry, my dearest one", he always said. "I have an awful lot to do. We can talk later." But that never happened.

One morning the King sat on his throne in the throne room once again and pondered. The new chocolate tax had been introduced. He ruled a United Kingdom, yet he was not satisfied and still didn't know why.

The door opened and General Brigadus came in.

"Hello, Your Majesty", he greeted the King in a good mood. He had slept long and had had a good breakfast. At breakfast, he had a splendid idea. He was in a particularly good mood.

"Good morning, General. I see you are well today."

Brigadus nodded. "Indeed. Because something occurred to me at breakfast. Something that will certainly cheer you up, your majesty. Something that will keep you occupied for a long time to come."

The King listened curiously. Something that would keep him occupied for some time? Something that would cheer him up? What could that possibly be? "Tell me, my dear general. What is this idea of yours?"

Brigadus teetered on his toes in delight. "Well, when I was having breakfast earlier, or more precisely, when I was about to eat my scrambled eggs, the scales fell from my eyes."

At this point a pause was made.

"Say it at once! What have you come up with?" exclaimed the King curiously.

"Well, I had ordered an extra-large portion of scrambled eggs. A mega-monster-sized portion, because I was very hungry. The egg was arranged on a plate. It was piled up into a mountain. It looked almost exactly like the hill on which your palace stands. Suddenly I had a vision. I saw a brand-new, magnificent palace." Again, the general was silent and looked at the King expectantly.

The King looked confused. "A palace on a hill of scrambled eggs? What is this?"

"Not just any palace. Your new palace, King Regulus. Have you not yet thought that now that you are ruling a United Kingdom, you need a new, more beautiful, more splendid and more distinguished palace than this one ...?". The general looked around disapprovingly before he spoke further. "This old, ramshackle, damp, ruined dump that you call a palace?"

"How - what?" The King rose from his throne. "How dare you call my palace an old ruin? You take that back right now, General! This palace was once home to my father and his father as well."

Although the King's face had turned all red with anger, General Brigadus kept calm. "There you have it. Your grandfather lived here before you. This palace is an old building. Wouldn't it be nice to live in a brand new, more modern palace? King Raj the Fifth of Mesopotunia also had a new palace built. Since he has been living there, he has become even more famous and even more important. Think, Sire. Don't you want to be important and famous too?"

"I would have no objection to that. But how is this to be done? A new palace will not be built on the site?", King Regulus thought. "It would also be nice to have a large, wide and magnificent road around the island from the palace. The new palace need not be on this hill. I'm tired of walking downhill anyway when I want to go to the harbour or to the village. Back to the palace I walk uphill and it is always so exhausting that I can hardly breathe when I reach the top. How many times I have thought and pondered how this could be changed. Unfortunately, I haven't come up with a solution yet."

General Brigadus was beaming. "Splendid, Your Majesty. A new palace and a magnificent road around the island. What a splendid idea. You may leave the planning to me. I'm not only a fabulous two-star general, I'm also a fine architect. I'll get right on it. But first, tell me how you envision your new palace and its magnificent street. And while we're at it: first of all, we'll build you a nice big Ship of State. That's what being King of a kingdom is all about."

A few days later, the people of Tavalu were amazed when the King's men began to cut down the trees that stood on the beach and dig up their roots. "There is to be a great, wide and magnificent road that runs around the island. A Ship of State will be built from the wood of these trees. There will also be a new palace. Thant's what King Regulus wants", they explained to the astonished people.
Because the people of Tavalu were used to being ruled by the King and not

to think for themselves, they shrugged their shoulders and went on with their business.

"King Regulus will know what is best", they said to themselves and did not worry any more. But that was about to change.

Chapter 9
Everybody has to pitch in

"That's not the way to do it, Your Majesty. We can't move fast enough!" General Brigadus stood before the King and had his hands on his hips. Again, the uniform stretched threateningly over his huge belly.

"I believe the general has grown even fatter. He shouldn't eat so many scrambled eggs", thought the King, but he did not utter the sentence. After all, General Brigadus had become the most important person for him, because he wanted to build him a Ship of State, a new palace and a road.

"What does that mean, my dear general?", he asked instead in a friendly manner.

"It means that we will not finish building until the winter storms begin. If that is the case, you will have to wait until next year before you can move into your new palace. Only the Ship of State is almost finished."

"Oh, no, I can't wait", cried the King indignantly. After all, he had already begun to pack his bags. If the building would take so long, he would have to unpack again and he didn't want that.

General Brigadus muttered his approval. "Exactly. That's not possible. That's why all the people of Tavalu must help. After all, it's important that the palace and the road be finished as soon as possible. By the way, we need more earth for the foundation and also more stones. If we take more earth and stones from this island, there will soon be no more hills or fields here."

"I see", nodded the King. "I will immediately pass a law which will state that all men on the island are to help build the palace and the road from now on. But as for the earth and stones, I do not know what to do."

"Once again, Your Majesty, I have a marvellous idea. After all, we live in a United Kingdom of Tavalu and Tuvala. It is only right that Tuvala helps us out with earth and stones when we have too few of them ourselves. After all, that is why they are ruled by you." The General clapped his hands with delight at his idea.

And so, it happened. All the men of Tavalu had to help build the palace and the road from now on, whether they wanted to or not. They grumbled and grumbled, but no one dared to contradict them, because the King's soldiers made sure that they worked hard. The women and children tilled the fields, but not very well. Life on Tavalu was suddenly quite exhausting.

But not only that. The King had barges built. They went to Tuvala and brought back a large quantity of stones and earth.

At first, the people of Tuvala were only surprised because they could not imagine what King Regulus wanted to do with all that earth and stones.

But when the ships didn't stop bringing earth and stones to Tuvalu, they became afraid. Full of horror they watched the excavators working all day long and making such a noise that they could not sleep a wink.

Finally, they went to Old Yuin to get some advice.

"What are we going to do?" they asked him helplessly. "Surely it can't be that King Regulus is taking away our land and our stones. Tuvala is getting smaller and smaller. If this continues, our island will disappear completely. Or else we will be left with rocks that we cannot live on."

"In general, the construction machines are so noisy that nobody can sleep during the day", said the others. "Then in the evening we are so tired that we can hardly drive up from sea. We almost fall asleep while fishing. That's dangerous of course, because you can easily fall into the water if you're not care-ful."

Amali had also come to Yuin with her parents. "You must know what to do. After all, you always know what to do", she exclaimed hopefully.

But Yuin shook his head sadly. "In this case I don't know what to do. I think King Regulus has gone mad. It probably has something to do with this general who is now advising him. I must disappoint you, Amali."

Then the people hung their heads and went home in silence. If wise Old Yuin didn't know what to do, no one could help them.

Only Amali stayed a while longer. She sat down next to Yuin. For a long time, they looked up at the sea.

Finally, Amali said softly, "You didn't let me down."

"I think so. After all, I don't know what to do", Yuin replied dejectedly. "I think you should go home now. The sun will go down soon, and your parents will be wondering where you are.

Amali got up. "I really believe you can still think of something we can do, Yuin. See you tomorrow."

Waving, she made her way home.

Chapter 10
Dreambird

When Amali came home, her parents sat together and did not even notice their daughter. Her mother was crying and her father had his arms wrapped around her.

"What are we going to do", sobbed her mother. "That crazy King and his fat general won't rest until they have taken our whole island to Tavalu. I've heard that the King is desperate for a new palace, and therefore needs all the earth. I'm so scared."

"It won't be so bad, dear", mumbled the father. Amali looked at him and saw that he too was afraid, but would not admit it. "It's dawning already. I must go out right away. I hope the fish bite tonight."

The mother sobbed up. "I'm afraid for you too. You couldn't sleep at all today because the excavators made such a racket again. What if you're so tired that you fall in the water."

"I can swim. I'll wake up in the cold water", smiled Amali's father.

Only now did the parents notice that Amali was at home. The mother quickly dried her eyes. "There you are, my little one." Lost in thought, she stroked her daughter's hair.

Later, when Amali was in bed, her mother came to her again. "Daddy has already gone out fishing", she said despondently.

"Please, Mama, don't cry. Yuin will find a solution. He just needs to think a while", Amali explained more firmly than she expected. She tried to be strong and brave, but in reality, she too was very scared.

"My big baby!" The mother kissed her on the forehead. "Sleep tight."

That night, Amali had a dream. She was standing on the beach looking out to sea. Suddenly a huge wave was coming at her. She tried in vain to run away. Her legs didn't obey her. But the wave got smaller and smaller until the water was just splashing around her feet. But what was that? A big golden stone shone in the shallow water. She wondered if the wave had washed it there. Curious, Amali waded towards it. Finally, she stood close to the stone and watched with fascination.

She was so busy that she didn't even notice the white bird that had been circling above her for a while. Finally, the bird sat down in the middle of the golden stone.

"Hello, Amali", he croaked and tilted his head, bird style.

Amali swallowed. Did the bird really talk to her? "Hello", she said tentatively.

"Isn't that amazing?" Somehow the bird looked like it was smiling. "I'm sure you've never talked to a bird before."

Amali told herself that this was only a dream and therefore decided not to be surprised. "Well, sometimes I've shouted something to a bird. The seagulls, for example, can be very loud and cheeky. But they never answered me. And I've never seen a bird like you before. How can you know my name?"

Now the bird gurgled with laughter, spread its wings and shook its feathers. "You're funny", he said after he finished laughing. "No wonder you've never seen one like me before. Because I am unique, because I am a dream bird. In fact, I'm your Dreambird." Again he put his head crooked and looked at her expectantly with his button eyes.

"A Dreambird? I have never heard of that", Amali explained. "Can you talk to me because you are my Dreambird? Can you do anything special? Will you visit me every night when I sleep?"

"Stop, stop, what a nosy little girl you are", the bird croaked. "We Dreambirds are something very special. We don't show ourselves to everyone, only to very special children in special moments."

Amali got big eyes. "Am I such a child? But I don't feel so special right now."

"I know. That's why I'm here. I felt your great fear, and I want to help you and your people." The bird picked at the stone with its beak. "Do you know what that is?"

"A rock?"

"That's right, a rock. But not just any stone, it's the Golden Sunstone. It had sunk long ago in the sea. Now it will soon surface to warn the people of these islands. "If they continue like this, one of these islands will soon be gone."

Frightened, Amali gasped for breath.

"No, no. You have nothing to be afraid of", the Dreambird tried to calm her down. "It's not the island you live on. I can see a bit into the future, but I see it as if through a thick fog. I don't know everything. But I do know that we must hurry. The people of the islands must unite and stop destroying their world. If they do that, all will be well."

"But we on our island do nothing at all", Amali explained indignantly. " It's the King of Tavalu! It's all his fault!"

The Dreambird croaked disapprovingly. "What do you mean 'our island'? The islands don't belong to someone. They belong to all the creatures that live there. Or they belong to nobody. It depends on how you look at it. It may be that the King of Tavalu has started destroying the islands, but all the people are joining in. No one tells him that it cannot continue or refuses to obey his orders. Someone has to talk to this King and make it clear to him that he cannot simply do what he wants. It takes a lot of courage, because he won't like to hear that."

Amali swallowed. "And you think that I'm... But I'm just a little girl. The King certainly won't listen to me."

"Then you must take someone the King listens to. Can you think of anyone like that?"

Amali was thinking. Suddenly she had an idea: "Yes, Yuin! He knows the Golden Sunstone and its history. I'll ask him to come with me. If the King doesn't listen to him, he will listen to no one else."

The Dreambird nodded contentedly. "This is a good plan, dear Amali. You shouldn't wait too long with it." He looked around. "But now I must fly. The dawn is already breaking in your world. Soon you will wake up. Farewell', with these words he swung himself into the air.

Amali looked at him. "Will you come to visit me again soon?" she asked a little sadly.

"We will meet again", replied the Dreambird. It was so quiet that Amelie hardly understood him, for he had almost disappeared between the clouds.

With a jerk, Amali sat up in her bed. She could almost hear the sound of the waves from her dream and feel the warm seawater on her legs. Dazed, she rubbed her eyes.

"Good morning, my little one", her mother greeted her as Amali came into the kitchen. "Daddy came home a while ago. He made a good catch. But now you must have breakfast first."

The mother did not seem as down this morning as she had been that evening. So Amali decided to talk to her about her dream.

"Mama", she began hesitantly. "Have you ever heard of the Golden Sunstone?"

The mother flinched in fright. "How do you know about this, Amali? There is an ancient story about the stone."

"I dreamed about the stone and a strange bird. A Dreambird..."

This is where Amelie's mother interrupted her. "You're imagining things. It's bad luck to talk about the Golden Sunstone because it's a bad omen. They say it will be bad luck if it appears. Please don't talk about it anymore. Now eat your breakfast, child."

So Amali preferred to be silent and decided to walk to Yuin right after breakfast and rather talk to him about her dream.

Chapter 11
The Golden Sunstone

"So, the bird of your dreams actually came to visit you?" Yuin looked thoughtfully at Amali. She immediately went to see him right after breakfast. As usual, he sat in front of his hut and looked at the sea. Amali had blurted out her story as soon as she sat down next to him. Yuin had listened to her attentively without interrupting her even once.

"Do you have a Dreambird, too?" Amali asked with big eyes.

Yuin smiled thoughtfully. "I did. You must know that Dreambirds only show themselves to children and only at certain moments. That is when the children are very afraid or very sad. Then their Dreambird comes to them at night in their sleep and comforts them. When the children grow up, the Dreambird no longer comes to them.

When I was a little boy, my parents died in a boating accident. As you can imagine, I was very sad about that. During this time, the Dreambird often came to me and comforted me. My aunt and uncle took me in like their own son. After a while I felt better. It wasn't that I wasn't still sad when I thought about my parents, but I could stand it."

"Poor you", Amali said softly. She couldn't imagine not having parents anymore.

Yuin smiled at her. "Thank you. But you know, it's been so long that I only think about my parents now and then. It's okay."

Amali nodded. Yuin was ancient, after all. She couldn't imagine him as a little boy at all. "I was not really comforted by my Dreambird. But he gave me some advice. Tell me, do you know anything about the Golden Sun Stone? Is that the stone from the story you wanted to tell the other day? My mother doesn't want to talk about it. She says it's bad luck."

"Of course. Everyone knows the story of the stone. But people don't like to talk about it", Yuin explained. "I want to tell you about the Stone:

A very long time ago, there was not only Tavalu and Tuvala, but a third island. It was called Tovali. It was bigger than the other two and much richer. People dressed in finest silk and ate and drank only the best. There was also a King. He loved gold and gems more than anything else. In the middle of this island stood the Golden Sunstone. How it got there, no one could say. It had been there as long as people could remember. When the sun shone on it, it looked as if it was made of pure gold. Once, as the King rode across the island, he passed the stone. The sun was high in the sky and the stone shone and glittered in splendour. When the

King saw this, he ordered the stone to be dug up and brought to him in the palace, because he wanted it all to himself. His order was carried out immediately. It took twenty strong men to dig up the stone and bring it to the palace, it was so big. But when the Golden Sunstone stood in the palace, it looked like an ordinary stone. It didn't shine a bit, because it needed the sunlight to sparkle. The King had a thousand candles lit, but even that didn't help. That made the King angry. He had the stone thrown into the deepest sea. Soon after, gold was found on Tovali. Because the King loved gold more than anything else, he ordered all the people to dig for it and deliver it to him in the palace. So, the people dug and dug and dug. Soon they had to dig deep tunnels to find more gold, and the island became completely hollow. Although the gold piled up in all the rooms of the palace, the King still did not have enough. One morning the Golden Sunstone was found on the beach, even though the King had had it thrown into the sea at the deepest point. Even more surprising was that the stone bore an inscription. It was a warning that the island would disappear into the sea if the King and his people went on like this. But the King did not take this seriously. Again, he ordered the stone to be sunk into the sea at the deepest point. During that night, a terrible storm arose. On Tavalu and Tuvala there was little sign of it. Only Tovali was badly affected by the wind and waves. The next morning there was nothing more to see of the island. It had disappeared into the sea with man and beast. Maybe it had soaked itself completely with water because the gold digging had made it as holey as a sponge. Since then, it has been said that the Golden Sunstone will rise again from the sea to warn people when they are as greedy as the King of Tovali."

Amali was thinking. "In my dream, I saw the Golden Sunstone. I'm sure it will turn up soon. We must go to Tavalu and warn King Regulus, as the Dreambird said. He must stop building and stealing our earth at once. You're coming with me, aren't you?"

"Of course, I'll come. I won't let you go to Tavalu by yourself. We can leave right now. My rowing boat is back there". With these words Yuin pointed to the beach where his little rowing boat lay.

"I have listened to you and this child because you are a wise man. Now you are telling me such nonsense. About some birds that appear in dreams and the ancient legend of the Golden Sunstone? There never was a third island. Those are all silly tales made up by old women. I don't have time for this. I've got to see if the people are working hard. My palace and the road are still not finished", King Regulus exclaimed angrily.

Amali and Yuin had rowed straight to Tavalu. From the harbour, they had gone to the palace and rung the bell. Minister Oops had opened the gate for them. When he heard that they wanted to see the King because they wanted to warn him, he had clapped his hands enthusiastically.

"At last, someone is coming who agrees with me. King Regulus no longer listens to me. He won't talk to me at all, no matter what I try. Come along. I'll take you to him. Perhaps you can persuade him. The opportunity is there because General Brigadus is not with him now."

In fact, he led them both to the throne room, where he knocked briefly and immediately opened the door. "Your Majesty, I'm sorry to disturb you. There is someone here who insists on speaking with you." Before King Regulus could answer, he had already pushed Yuin and Amali into the throne room.

"It is a mistake not to believe us, Lord King. Something bad will happen. Please do not let any more stones or earth be taken from our island. The forest will grow thin, all the plants will suffer, and so will the people. The people are slowly getting afraid that Tuvala will disappear completely one day", Yuin said, without being intimidated by the King.

King Regulus laughed angrily. "Don't be like that. Why do you need a forest? You are a fishing people. You can't use stones anyway, and earth is useless to you, just like trees."

When he heard this, Yuin realized that the King would not listen to him. "You will regret not having listened to us, Lord King. Soon the Golden Sunstone will be found on Tavalu beach. Perhaps by then it will be too late."

He turned to Amali. "Come, let's go. We have no business here anymore."

Despondent, Amali took his hand and the two of them set off for the harbour to row back to Tuvala.

Chapter 12
A bad omen

King Regulus did not care about the warning from Yuin and Amali. On the contrary! He made his people work harder and harder because he wanted to move into his palace before the rainy season.

Even though General Brigadus was at the construction site all day, driving the people on, it was not fast enough for King Regulus. The King always had something to criticize. Once, he thought the people were lazy and stupid. Another time a wall of the palace was not built straight enough for him and it had to be torn down again. The magnificent street was sometimes not magnificent and then again not wide enough. More and more often the King shouted around and blamed General Brigadus for everything.

Finally, the general got fed up with always being scolded by the King. He secretly got his sailing ship ready for departure.

One day, when the wind was favourable, he boarded the ship, raised the sails and sailed away.

He left a letter for the King:

Dear King Regulus.
I regret to inform you that I've been in Tavalu long enough So I'm sailing away now, because I must continue on my important mission. Emperor Raj the Fifth is counting on me!
Your Ship of State is ready, the palace and the street will be handed over to you shortly.
All built just for you.

If I may give you one more piece of advice: If the construction work takes too long, let the people of Tuvala help you. After all, they are all your subjects, so you can control them.

Yours sincerely

General Brigadus
Delegate
from
Raj the Fifth
Emperor of Mesopotunia

When the King had read this message, he became so angry that he tore it into thousand shreds and threw it out of the window.

"Who does that fat general think he is?", he shouted angrily. "Now that I urgently need help to finish my new palace, he just sails away!"

Minister Oops rushed to the throne room. "Your Majesty!" he gasped.

"You're just what I needed, Oops", the King bellowed. "Why are you panting? Is something wrong with my new palace? Have those stupid peasants put up another wall crooked again? So speak up!"

Minister Oops took a deep breath. "It will be best if you come down to the harbour with me."

"What am I doing there?" the King asked in surprise. "The construction site is somewhere else."

"It has nothing to do with the new palace. Come quickly. Something has been washed up!"

Minister Oops turned around and waved for the King to follow him.

Astonished, King Regulus went to port with him.

A lot of people had gathered here. They were standing around an object that could not be recognized.

"Make way for the King", cried Minister Oops loudly. In fact, the people formed an alley for King Regulus.

He quickly walked towards the object. He was startled. In front of him lay a large stone glistening golden in the sun.

"The Golden Sunstone", the King stammered.

"The Golden Sunstone", the people repeated reverently and fearfully.

"Look, sire, there's something written on the stone", exclaimed one of the people. It was true. In the middle of the stone was an inscription.

It read...

Beware!
If this stone sinks into the sea again then the people have violated the immutable laws of the sea and will therefore severely punished for all time.

King Regulus flinched.
The Golden Sunstone was real! He had always laughed at the old stories and not taken them seriously. Now the

stone lay before him and glittered and gleamed in the sunlight. If the stone really existed, then the warning that the wise man and the child had given should be true? He turned to his first minister.

"I want you to go to Tuvala and bring the wise man and the child who was with him the other day."

"You there", he pointed to the people who continued to surround the stone and marvel at it. "You carry this stone to the palace. There you will bring it to the highest pinnacle. The sea will never rise that high. That is why the stone can never sink again. Let's see who is the wisest here."

Everyone followed the King's orders. Minister Oops left for Tuvala.

Meanwhile, the people moved the Golden Sunstone to the highest pinnacle of the palace. "Our King is clever", they said among themselves. "The sea will never come up here."

Chapter 13
Money cannot be eaten

Minister Oops had rowed to Tuvala as fast as he could. He went straight to Yuin and told him that the Golden Sunstone had washed up in Tavalu harbor and that the King wanted to see him and Amali.

"What does the fat general say?" Yuin asked curiously.

Oops grinned. "He's run away. He was fed up with being scolded by King Regulus all the time when something didn't work out the way the King wanted it to. He and his crew sneaked onto his sailing ship and took off."

"We will not miss him! Come on, Oops, let's get Amali and go to the King. Maybe now he'll come to his senses."

So Yuin and Minister Uups set off. Luckily, Amali was just home. She had decided to help her mother a little today, to cheer her up, because her mother was still desperate and sad because she feared that all the earth would be brought to Tavalu and only rocks would remain. When she heard that Amali was to come to King Regulus, she wrung her hands in horror. "What does the King want with my little one?", she exclaimed.

Yuin patted her shoulder. "You need not fear for Amali. I will take good care of her. Amali is a very special girl, you should know that."

Together with Minister Oops, Yuin succeeded in calming the mother, so that she agreed to let Amali go.

Soon they stood before the King. He beckoned them to follow him. "Come, I want to show you something."

They went up to the highest pinnacle of the palace. There King Regulus pointed to the Golden Sunstone. "Surely you have heard that the stone has been washed up. I had it brought here immediately. That's particularly clever and cunning of me. It will never sink in the sea again."

Yuin watched the stone closely while Amali ran her fingers along the inscription. "It looks just like in my dream", she murmured. "Maybe even a bit more golden and beautiful."

"Do you believe us now, King Regulus?" Yuin asked. "The old prophecy is true. The warning written on the Golden Sunstone is also true. You should take it seriously and stop destroying the islands, just because you want a new, bigger and more beautiful palace and a useless road. Besides, it won't matter how high you set the stone. It will always find its way back into the sea if it has to. So says the prophecy."

"Rubbish! The sea will never rise that high! I'm sure of it", King Regulus declared, gritting his teeth to a smile. He looked a bit like a shark now. "Nevertheless, I have decided to have no more earth and stones brought over from Tuvala."

"Really?" Yuin looked suspiciously at the King. He couldn't imagine that the King would abandon his plan. "Don't you need any more earth or stones? Is the palace finally finished?"

"Not yet. Unfortunately, it is far from being finished. Nevertheless, in the future we will use our own stones for building again. Because it is much too complicated to always cross over to your place. We have the few stones we need ourselves.

Yuin didn't trust the King. "It's not logical", he said, "if it's too much trouble to come to us, you could have taken your own stones and your own earth from the beginning. Go ahead and say what you want!"

King Regulus examined him cunningly. "You're a smart lad, old man. Not for nothing you are the wise man of Tuvala. I've had an idea. How would it be if the men of Tuvala helped build my palace and I would pay them well. They don't have to build on this magnificent road. If they work on the palace, that would be enough for me." The King had remembered what General Brigadus had advised him in his farewell letter. But he did not want to admit that this was not his idea, so he pretended to have thought of it himself.

Yuin shook his head. "None of the men will do that. We are a nation of fisher-men and make our living by having the men go out to sea at night and cast their nets. In the morning they will come back. Then they have to sleep because they have worked all night. No one will want to go over to Tavalu to work on the palace."

"But I pay you good money for your work. You get more than my other workers!"

Yuin shook his head again. But before he could say anything, Amali answered the King, "What should we do with it? We eat from the fish the men catch. Vegetables and fruits grow in our gardens. My parents made my toys for me. When we want something, we do not need money, we simply exchange things for other things. That's why we don't need money in Tuvala! We can't eat money, we can't play with it, we can't use it for anything!"

"This is incredible! What a stubborn people you are in Tuvala", the King rumbled. "You must help build the palace, after all, you are my subjects. Subjects must obey their King. Otherwise I will send my soldiers and teach you to obey."

"Are you threatening us, Mr. King?" Yuin looked at the King with evil eyes. "Haven't you done enough to us already. You should be ashamed of yourself!"

Again the King grinned like a shark. "Why should I? It is my right. Go back to your island and talk to the men. They have to work for me, or you'll all get into serious trouble. As sure as I am King Regulus."

The King was very serious, Yuin and Amali saw it the same way. They looked at each other in despair. What would happen if the men were forced to work for the King and could no long-er go fishing?

Chapter 14
Yuin has a plan

"Believe me, my dear Yuin, King Regulus was not like this in the old days. He changed when the General showed up and put flea in his ear! I've tried to reason with the King, but he won't listen to me. Now the general is gone and the King is still like this - uum...", Minister Oops faltered. He actually didn't want to say anything bad about King Regulus.

"Mean? Sneaky? Mean and nasty?" Amali finished the sentence.

"You must believe me, this is not the Regulus I know. I don't know what has got into him either. I do hope he comes to his senses soon. Until then, it is better for you and your people to do as the King commands. Once he arrives in Tuvala with his soldiers, it will be too late." Minister Oops said the last sentence very quietly, because he was secretly ashamed of his King.

The three sat together in Minister Oops boat. He brought Amali and Yuin back to Tuvala. Yuin didn't seem to have listened at all. He stared at the water, lost in thought. Suddenly, he snapped his fingers. "I got it", he exclaimed happily.

"What?", Amali asked.

"How?", exclaimed Minister Oops.

Yuin beamed at her. "I just thought of something. I have to think about it a bit more. When we get to Tuvala, you will know what it is."

They hurried to get to the small island quickly. Here Yuin called everyone to him. They sat around him in a circle. He told them what had happened. That the King wanted the men to work for him and that he would pay them a lot of money for it. And that King Regulus did not want any more earth or stones taken from Tuvala.

There was uproar.

"That the King wants to take his own stones from now on is fine, but we will not work for him", the people exclaimed indignantly. "We are fishermen, not construction workers. What do we have to do with his money, we don't need any? Let him leave us alone!"

"Listen to me!" Yuin raised his hands and the people fell silent. "We will have no choice but to work for the King. Otherwise he will send his soldiers after us. What that means, I'm sure everyone can imagine for themselves."

When the people heard that King Regulus wanted to send soldiers, they were terrified. But Yuin spoke quickly to calm them down. "I have thought of something. How about we accept his offer? Soon the rainy season will begin and with it the winter storms. We only work for the King for a few weeks. But we won't take money for it. We claim our earth back. The stones he can keep, but the earth of Tuvala he must give back to us. It is more precious than any money."

People agreed with that. They wanted nothing more than to have their island back the way it was. The very next morning the men went to Tavalu and reported for work. King Regulus was pleased. He and his men laughed at the men from Tuvala because they didn't want money, only earth as payment. But he allowed them to take as much earth as they could store in their ships to Tuvala.

Now a hard time began for the people of Tuvala. Because the men worked all day on the big island, they were so tired in the evening that they hardly ever went out fishing. The women and children had to do everything alone.

There was just enough food to feed everyone. Still, the people didn't lose heart. They knew that the men would not work on the big island for long. In the evening, the men brought their boats full of earth to Tuvala, the women and children spread them out and planted flower seeds over them.

On Tavalu, the people were not well either. The women and children were still cultivating the fields. The harvest was not good. That's why there was hardly enough to eat. The people grumbled, but they still didn't dare to speak their mind out loud. King Regulus now had stones broken out of the hill on which his old palace stood, so that the hill soon looked all holey. But that didn't bother the King at all. "Soon I will live in my new, beautiful and magnificent palace. What do I care if the hill has holes in it? I won't need them or the old palace anymore!"

116

Chapter 15
The earth is trembling

For a few weeks men from the small island worked for King Regulus, then it started to rain. It got colder, the sun hid more and more behind thick clouds. The rainy season had come. The palace was almost finished, only the roof was missing.

One morning it rained especially hard, with enormous storms. Huge waves were breaking on the beach of the two islands. The men from the small island decided not to go to Tuvala. They would not do so until the wind and waves had calmed down.
"My father says that the King cannot demand that the men go to Tavalu in this weather. The crossing is much too dangerous", Amali said to Yuin. She had walked to him in a short break

from the rain. Now they were sitting in Yuin's hut, drinking sweet tea.

Yuin nodded. "Your father is right. It's better not to go out in this wind. By the way, it's no longer necessary for the men to continue working at the new palace. Firstly, the palace is almost finished, and secondly, we've retrieved almost all of our earth." He took a thoughtful sip from his teacup. "All we have to do is figure out a way to make the King understand that we no longer work for him."

"He won't understand that", a voice was heard. Minister Oops stood in the doorway. He clung trembling to the door frame. But what did he look like? He was wet and dishevelled. His face had taken on a greenish colour.

Yuin quickly went over to him. "My dear Oops, what happened to you? Are you sick? Why are you even here?"

While Minister Oops lowered himself onto a chair, Amali poured him a cup of hot tea.

"Thank you", the minister sighed and took a sip. "That feels good. I'm frozen stiff. The crossing to here was hell. I thought the boat would sink any moment. It's all horrible. I'm here by order of the King. He's furious because the men didn't show up to work today. But that is not the worst thing", here Minister Uups swallowed heavily. "The Golden Sunstone..."

Yuin had jumped up. "What about the stone?" he shouted excitedly. "It's not..."

"Yes, it is", muttered the minister. "We had a terrible storm tonight. The wind roared and roared and the waves roared higher and higher. Nobody could believe what happened. The wind blew the Golden Sunstone from the highest pinnacle of the palace and the waves took it away. Now it has sunk into the sea. King Regulus has given me orders to come here and take you both to Tavalu. I am to tell the men to report for work in the morning, or the King will come here with his soldiers."

"Then let him come with his soldiers", Yuin exclaimed grimly. "That's enough now! I don't even think about going to Tavalu in this storm, and certainly not with Amali. It's much too dangerous." As if the wind wanted to confirm his exclamation, it howled and raged around Yuin's hut.

"We'd better get ready for a sleepless night. Minister Oops can stay at my place. It seems you won't be able to return to Tavalu tonight. You're lucky that you made it safely to us. Make yourself comfortable. I'll take Amali home. She can't possibly go home alone in this storm."

When the Golden Sunstone had sunk into the sea, the people of Tavalu had guessed that it would come to a bad end. Even the elders among them could not remember ever having experienced such a storm.

"This is all happening because King Regulus wanted a new palace. Why couldn't he be happy with his old palace? For weeks we've been slaving away for him, the fields are not being cultivated properly, there's not enough food", they grumbled and moaned and locked themselves up in their houses in fear. There they wanted to wait until the great storm was over. But instead of moving on or calming down, the storm only got stronger and stronger and worse. It raged incessantly and ever more strongly on the whole island. It was accompanied by hailstones as big as eggs. They crashed into streets and house roofs, smashed windows and flowerpots and devastated the fields.

When evening came, the earth began to shake.

That's when people became even more afraid. They ran out of their houses because they were afraid that the houses would collapse.

"To the harbour! Let's go out to sea. Our island is bound to sink, as it happened to Tovali", someone shouted. When they heard that, all the people ran to the harbour to get on a ship. In no time at all, the ships cast off and went out to sea. From here, the people saw that the mountain where King Regulus' old castle stood collapsed. Soon nothing was left of the harbour, the mountain and the castle but a huge heap of rubble.

"Oh dear, where shall we go now?" cried the people.

"That's easy, we'll go to Tuvala", said a well-known voice.

"The King! He lives! He has not been buried under the rubble of the palace!" muttered the people.

When the earth began to tremble, even King Regulus had feared that the island would sink in the sea. That's why he ran to the harbour, like everyone else. There he had gone straight to his new Ship of State and had made sure that as many people as possible got on the ship. Now his ship took the lead and everyone else followed him.

Chapter 16
After the storm

The further the ships moved away from Tavalu, the less stormy it became. When they finally arrived on the small island, the wind had almost completely died down. They anchored in the harbour.

"It will be best to go ashore. Who knows if the storm won't come here too? Then it's better to have solid ground under your feet", the King explained.

So, the people did. There was quite a crowd on the pier. Reluctantly, the people of Tuvala came out of their houses. How astonished they were when they saw that their port was full of ships and that the people of Tavalu were crowding around King Regulus on the pier.

Finally, Yuin and Minister Oops came to the harbour. Yuin examined the King coldly. "You are not welcome here!"

The people from the small island murmured approvingly.

"But, but, my dear subjects", blustered the King. "I can understand that you are a little upset. But we are the United Kingdom of Tavalu and Tuvala, and I am your King. Therefore, you must help us now. A great storm has come over Tavalu. The earth shook and the mountain with my palace on it collapsed."

"As holey as the mountain has become, it's no wonder. We had to get stones for the new palace from there", exclaimed one man.

The King overheard this interjection. "As I said, the mountain has collapsed and has buried the harbour underneath it. We will live here on Tuvala from now on", he said.

"Stop!" Minister Oops took a step towards the King. "I have kept silent long enough. Now it is over. That this all happened is entirely your fault, King Regulus. Why did you suddenly need a new palace? Why this great street that no one wants and needs but you? You let General Brigadus put a flea in your ear. He ran away when the going got tough. Anyway, what is this nonsense: the United Kingdom of Tavalu and Tu-vala! The people here don't want to be ruled by you at all. You have already caused enough trouble. Enough is enough!"

"Hear, hear", shouted the people of Tuvala and also the people of the big island nodded. They, too, were fed up with being ruled by King Regulus.

"Oops, you get to the point", Yuin said. "We don't want a King here. Especially one who only thinks of himself and not his people."

King Regulus had listened with his mouth open. "But, but... I am your King", he stammered.

"Pah, you have never been our King"
and "Go away and leave us alone",
cried the people of Tuvala.

" We do not want a King who wants to
enslave us for his palace ", cried the
people of Tavalu.

"I hope you finally understand. You are
not our King, and you can take your
Kingdom elsewhere ", Yuin explained.

"You should realize what you have
done! This is unforgivable and that's
why I resign. Why don't you find yourself another first minister?", Oops added determinedly.

"Are you against me too, Minister
Oops? You no longer want to be my
first minister? What shall I do without
you?" King Regulus hung his head. "I
admit I have done wrong of late. I'm
very sorry. But I am alone responsible
for it. Please help my subjects", he interrupted. "I mean, help the people of
Tavalu. They cannot return to the island for the time being. If you don't

want me here, then I'll get on my ship and leave immediately. Anywhere. I won't have a home anymore." He wiped away a tear sadly.

Even though the King had done so many things wrong and her parents had been sad so often because of him, Amali could not see it. She went to King Regulus and took his hand. "Surely you don't have to go away, Lord King", she said.

Yuin nodded. "Of course, we will help. You can stay here if you want to, King Regulus. However, only if it is clear that you have no say here. Now let us first see where we can put you all. Tomorrow morning we'll go to Tavalu and see what it looks like there. Maybe it's not all that bad."

So it happened. The people of Tuvala welcomed the refugees from the great island. After all, it wasn't their fault that their King had gone mad. King Regulus went with Yuin and Oops to

Yuin's hut. Here he was first given a hot tea to warm himself up. The three of them talked together until late at night. Little by little the King realized that he had done wrong and he was very sorry. The next morning, they all went to Tavalu together. The storm had raged there much worse than on Tuvala; also an earthquake had never happened on the island before. Many things were broken, the mountain and the palace had buried the harbour under their rubble. Yet everyone was glad that the island had not sunk into the sea, as the prophecy said. Also, the new palace had collapsed.

Immediately everyone set out to re-move the rubble, to rebuild collapsed houses and to replant the fields.

It was quite a job, but the people were happy to do it. The people from the small island helped wherever they could.

There was only one thing that wasn't rebuilt: King Regulus' palace. But the King wasn't angry or sad about that. He understood that it was not about living in a great, magnificent palace and ruling the people, but about helping and understanding each other. He decided not to be King anymore and to live in a normal house. He just let the people decide for themselves how they wanted to live.

Minister Oops helped the people of Tavalu, just as Yuin had been doing on the small island for years and days. It worked out fantastically. Suddenly the people of Tavalu had time to sing and dance and not just work all the time and they liked that very much.

Once a year the people from the big and small islands met. One year on Tavalu and the other year on Tuvala. Then they celebrated with a big party together. Even Regulus, who was no longer a King, could not resist joining in the celebration.

While he ate delicious fried fish, drank homemade apple juice and cheerfully watched the people, he thought each time, "How lucky I am that I no longer have to rule."

Chapter 17
See you soon, Amali

That night Amali dreamt again that she was standing on the beach. But unlike her first dream, there wasn't a big wave coming at her. Warm water washed around her ankles. The wind caressed her gently. There was a roar. With a small hop, the Dreambird settled down next to her.

"Hello, Amali", he croaked as when they met first.

Amali sat down next to him and gently stroked his plumage. "Hello, Dreambird."

"I told you we would meet again", said the bird.

"I am glad. Will you come to visit me more often now?" Amali asked curiously.

The bird shook so that the feathers flew, just like that. "I don't think so. Because you don't need me anymore.

As I told you before, I can see a bit into the future. To you, I see only beautiful things. I'm sure you're going to have problems from time to time, but you're doing fine on your own. That's why I want to say goodbye to you."

"But I had been looking forward to meeting you in my dreams every now and then", Amali said sadly.

"Look, we Dreambirds are there to help children who are afraid and unwell. That's why we don't have so much time." The Dreambird hopped from one leg to the other. "You must understand this, dear Amali."

"What a pity. Maybe you'll find time to come and visit me sometime anyway. I'd like that very much."

"Hm, maybe I'll make an exception for you", the Dreambird spread its wings and -whoosh - it floated in the air.

"I think I will indeed visit you again, although you will never be so afraid again", Amali heard him croak. Or was

it the wind rustling in her ears? She
stood up and waved at her Dreambird.

At this point I would like to say thank you:

Dear Jill,
I would like to thank you very much. Without you and your review I would not have been able to translate this book into English and publish it. There is still so much to learn if you want to translate a book into another language - and I am glad that you are doing all the work to help me, to support me and to turn my bumpy English into something worth reading. It is so nice to have friends!
Thanks

My dear Rudi, I also thank you for everything. What should I do without you ...

Text and idea: Angie Pfeiffer

Translation: Rudi
(along with his MacBook)

Proofreading and editing: Jill Luke

Angie Pfeiffer, was born in 1955 in Gelsen-kirchen. She writes light fiction in the form of novels and short stories for adults as well as children's books. She has published novels, e-books and numerous short stories in anthologies, literary magazines and the daily press.

Home: angie-pfeiffer.com

Who will save Tricolour Country

Every morning, just before sunrise, King Fabulus from Tricolour Country climbs to the highest pinnacle of his castle and raises his red, yellow and blue ringed magic wand. Then a thick beam of paint is released from its tip, bringing the colours to the people. But one day wizard Shadowraven steals the magic wand. He cannot stand bright colours and wants the whole world to look grey. Immediately, King Fabulus takes off in a hot air balloon to retrieve the wand. He soon finds out that three children from Tricoulor Country have smuggled themselves into his balloon. They want to help the King to get back the wand.